For My Children

Written by V. Moua

Hello ladies and gentlemen. Are you ready to see some magic!

The Great Sammy
(that's me)
will be your magician.

Prepare to be amazed!

For my first trick,
I will pull a rabbit
out of this hat.

Abracadabra!

See! What did I tell you.

Wait a minute...
that's not a rabbit.
That's a snake!

Aaaahhhh!
I want my mommy!

That was a close one.

But I think you'll like
my next magic trick.

I'm going to saw
my dog in half and
put him back together.

Don't worry Spot,
this won't hurt one bit.

Kids, don't try
this at home.
I am a trained
magician.

Spot, come back!

WOOF!
WOOF!

That didn't go so well.

I need another volunteer—
for a different magic trick.

How about you?

Think of a number
between one and a million.
Can you do that for me?

Did you think of a number yet?

The number you're thinking of is...

NOT zero!

Am I right?

Am I a great magician or what?

What?
You're not impressed?

Are you ready?
One...
two...

three—

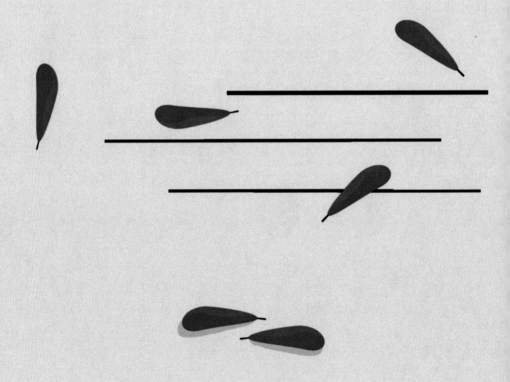

How did you know
where I was hiding?

Okay, I saved the
best trick for last.

I'm going to free myself
from this straitjacket...

and I'm going to do
it in five seconds!

Please count to five
and then turn the page.

Hey, you're cheating!
You didn't count to five yet.

Give me five more seconds...please!

Eee-yah!

Ooo-yah!

Why can't I get out of this!

Can you help me?
PRETTY PLEASE!

Where are you going?
Don't leave me like this!

At least turn off the
lights on your way out.

Goodbye.

The End

Visit the author's website:

http://vmoua.com

Made in the USA
Middletown, DE
25 October 2022

13522089R00027